PETITE ROUGE

A Cajun Red Riding Hood

MIKE ARTELL

ILLUSTRATED BY JIM HARRIS

DIAL BOOKS FOR YOUNG READERS · NEW YORK

Published by Dial Books for Young Readers

A division of Penguin Putnam Inc.

345 Hudson Street

New York, New York 10014

Text copyright © 2001 by Mike Artell

Illustrations copyright © 2001 by Jim Harris

Designed by Lily Malcom

Text set in Granjon

Printed in Hong Kong on acid-free paper

10 9 8 7 6 5 4 3 2 1

Library of Congress Cataloging-in-Publication Data

Artell, Mike.

Petite Rouge: a Cajun Red Riding Hood / Mike Artell;

illustrated by Jim Harris.

p. cm.

Summary: In this Cajun version of "Little Red Riding
Hood," the big bad gator is no match for a sharp young
girl and her quick-thinking cat.

ISBN 0-8037-2514-0

[1. Fairy tales. 2. Folklore. 3. Stories in rhyme.] I. Harris,
Jim, date, ill. II. Title.

PZ8.3.A685 Pe 2001

398.2'089'410763—dc21

[E]   99-087550

The full-color artwork was prepared using
watercolor and pencil on Stathmore rag bristol.

*A little mouse is hiding on every spread of this
book . . . see how many of them you can find.*

A BRIEF HISTORY OF THE CAJUN PEOPLE

In the mid-1750's, a group of French-speaking people lived in an area of Canada known as French Acadia, which was then ruled by the English government. Officials of the English government informed the Acadians that they were required to pledge their allegiance to the King of England. Being loyal to France, the Acadians refused. As a result, the Acadians were forced by English officials to board boats that would take them to America. About 800 or 900 of the Acadians boarded the boats and landed near Washington, D.C. Most, however, made the long trip to Louisiana, which had a large French-speaking population at the time. Many of these "Cajuns" (a corruption of the word "Acadians") moved inland and settled along the shores of Bayou Teche near Lafayette, where they can be found to this day.

DEDICATIONS

Through the years, the culture of the Cajun people has continued to grow rich in food, music, religious tradition, and the love of life. Both of my parents were born and raised in southwest Louisiana, my mother in Lafayette, and my father in Melville, near Opelousas. As a young boy, I heard many wonderful stories about the Cajun people and their legendary sense of humor. I dedicate this book to all those who continue to preserve and enhance that very special culture. —M.A.

To Little Brookie and her beloved cat. —J.H.

GLOSSARY

In this story, you may find some words that are new to you. Here's what they mean:

Adieu—pronounced "ah DYUH," this word means "good-bye."

Boudin—pronounced "BOO dan," it is a kind of Cajun sausage.

Etouffeé—pronounced "ay too FAY," this word literally means "smothered." Food that is prepared in this manner is covered with liquid while it cooks.

Filé—pronounced "FEE lay," it is a seasoning made of ground sassafras root.

Grand-mère—pronounced "grawnd mare," it is the French term for Grandmother.

Gumbo—pronounced "GUM bo," it is a kind of Cajun soup that includes okra, chicken, sausage, or seafood. The word gumbo is an African Bantu word that means "okra."

Mais oui—pronounced "may WEE," it is the French term for "yes."

Pirogue—pronounced "PEE rowg," it is a narrow, flat canoe that is pushed or paddled through the bayou, marsh, or swamp.

Si'l vous plaît—pronounced "seal voo PLAY," it is the French term for "If you please."

Back in de swamp
where dat Spanish moss grow,
I heard me a story
from long time ago.

In a little ol' house
dat been built outta wood,
live a girl people call
Petite Rouge Riding Hood.

One day, when her grand-mère
come down wit' de flu,
Petite Rouge mama tol' her
what she got to do.

"Take her dis gumbo
an' t'ree or two sweater.
An' some uh dis boudin
gone make her feel better.

"You can take de pirogue
wit' dat big long push pole,
den dere's jus' one mo' t'ing
dat you need to be tol'.

"Don' stop in de swamp!
Don' you stop on de way!
'Cause de swamp's fulla gators,
Cher! Dat's where dey stay!

"So you take dat cat
in de pirogue wit' you.
An' bring youself home
jus' as soon as you t'roo."

Petite Rouge take dat food,
an' her cat TeJean too,
den jump in dat pirogue
like she tol' to do.

Mama wave adieu
an', TeJean, he wave back,
as he float t'roo de swamp
where de water look black.

Dey don' be gone long
when dey see by a stomp,
a big, long, green log
dat got plenty a' bomp.

Dat log, it come close
to de pirogue and say,
"Now what you two doin' out here . . .
si'l vous plaît?"

It was Claude, dat ol' gator.
Petite Rouge gotta honch
dat ol' Claude t'inkin' he'd
like to have her fo' lonch.

"We takin' dis food to mah
grand-mère's," she say.
"An' I got me dis pole,
so you git out de way!"

"Pardon, mad'moiselle,
 I don' mean to be rude.
 I jus' t'inkin' dat maybe
 you share some you food.

"A taste a' dat boudin
 or shrimp etouffeé.
 Dat's all dat I want,
 den I'll git out de way."

Petite Rouge raise dat pole
 way up high in de air,
 an' she look at ol' Claude,
 an' she give him a stare.

"I'm countin' to t'ree,
 an' if you still dere,
 dis pole gonna hit you
 where you part you hair."

An' when she say, "One,"
 Ol' Claude back out de way.
 He know dat de girl
 sho' 'nuff mean what she say.

Den li'l Petite Rouge
push dat pirogue ag'in.
An' ol' Claude close his eyes.
An' ol' Claude start to grin.

"I got an idea
an' I know what to do.
I'll get me dat food
an' dat li'l girl too!"

Dat gator swim fast,
an' den quick as dem mouse,
he up on de porch of
Grand-mère's ol' house.

He open de door and
den stick in his head.
An' den he see Grand-mère
asleep in de bed.

He try to tiptoe
so she don' hear no sound,
but his tail bomp de shelf
an' two cup fall down.

When dey hit de floor (CRASH!),
it break bot' dem cup.
An' Grand-mère, she hear it.
An' Grand-mère wake up. . . .

"Sacre!" she exclaim.
"I know dis ain't right!"
Den she run in de closet
an' lock dat door tight!

"Ha! Ha!" ol' Claude laugh.
"You can hide; dat's okay.
In fac', it's mo' better
wit' you out de way."

Claude put on de nightgown
an' Grand-mère's nightcap,
den jomp in de bed
like he takin' a nap.

He pull up de covers round
his big ol' green head
an' pretend dat he's Grand-mère
jus' lyin' in bed.

An' sho' 'nuff, right soon
dere's a knock at de door,
an' Claude say, "Come in. . . .
What you stay outside fo'?"

An' in walk TeJean
an' Petite Rouge Riding Hood.
An' dey look at dat Grand-mère,
an' she don' look good.

Petite Rouge, she say, "Grand-mère!
You face! It's all green!
An' you skin got dem bomps.
Now what do dat mean?"

Ol' Claude make a smile,
an' he say, "It's dat flu.
It make me all green wit' dem bomps,
dat's fo' tru'.

"Why don' you come closer,
'cause I wanna see
all dat good food you mama
done cook fo' po' me."

Petite Rouge Riding Hood
an' den TeJean de cat,
dey take a step closer
from where dey was at.

Petite Rouge, she say, "Grand-mère!
I know you been sick,
but I t'ink mah eyes
be playin' on me a trick.

"You mout' kinda big,
 an' you nose kinda long,
 an' I got me a feelin'
 dat somet'in' bad wrong."

"I been rubbin' mah nose
 wit' dem tissue," say Claude,
"an' mah nose look fonny
 'cause I rub it too hard.

"Now come one step closer,"
    say Claude kinda sweet,
"'cause I t'inkin' dat maybe
    it's 'bout time to eat."

Petite Rouge and TeJean
    get up real close.
When Claude smile,
    TeJean turn as white as dem ghos'.

Petite Rouge, she say, "Grand-mère!
    You teeth big and white!
An' TeJean an' me know
    dat somet'in' ain't right."

An' dat's when Claude laugh,
    an' he say, "Oh. . . . Mais oui!
It ain't right fo' you,
    but it sho' right fo' me!"

Claude t'ro off dem sheet.
Petite Rouge shout, "*Aiieee!*
It's dat gator who wanna
make lonch outta me!"

Claude crawl out de bed
an' den onto de floor.
Den Petite Rouge know she
got some trouble, fo' sho'!

But TeJean de cat, ya'll,
he know what to do.
He smart fo' a cat.
Yeah, you know dat fo' tru'.

When Claude turn his back,
TeJean run to de table
an' jump up on top
jus' as fas' as he able.

He find him de bottle
dat say "Red Hot Sauce."
Den he reach back his arm
an' he give it a toss.

He see Petite Rouge
catch de sauce in her han',
den he pull out dat basket
a piece a' boudin.

He toss dat boudin
jus' when Claude start to hiss.
TeJean cross his fingers
an' hope she don' miss.

Petite Rouge watch dat boudin
come fly t'roo de air,
den she reach up an' catch it . . .
but guess who right dere?

Dat's right! It was Claude.
Petite Rouge knew one t'ing:
Ol' Claude's mout' ain't open
'cause he like to sing!

She take dat hot sauce
and 'fo' you count to two,
she soak dat boudin wit' dat sauce,
t'roo and t'roo.

She shove dat boudin right
in front a' Claude's nose,
jus' 'bout de same time
Claude done snap his jaws close.

He t'ink he done bite
Petite Rouge Riding Hood,
an', at firs', Claude be t'inkin'
she taste pretty good.

But den he stop chewin'
an' close bot' his eye,
den sit up and t'ink
maybe he gonna die!

He make dem back flip
'cause dat boudin so hot.
An' de next t'ing you know,
his tail tied in dem knot!

He dance all around.
He don' know what to do.
His mout' feel like fire.
His nose burnin' too.

So into de swamp
wit' his mout' open wide,
Claude jomp in dat water
to cool off inside.

An' den, from dat closet,
Grand-mère, she peek out,
'cause she want to see
what be makin' Claude shout.

An' when she see Claude
in dat swamp jompin' roun',
she come out de closet
an' dance up and down.

Den Grand-mère, TeJean, an'
Petite Rouge Riding Hood
be roll' on dat floor
an' dey laugh deyself good.

Den Grand-mère stan' up
an' she dus' off her clothes.
She say, "Hoo! Dat food sho'
smell good to mah nose.

"Now pull up some chair
an' le's take a look
at all a' de good food
you mama done cook."

An' soon, dey all eatin'
dat shrimp etouffeé,
boudin, an' gumbo
wit' lotsa filé.

An' when dey all t'roo,
Petite Rouge tell Grand-mère,
"Go sit youself down
in you big rockin' chair."

Grand-mère, she sit down
wit' TeJean on her lap,
an' soon Petite Rouge and
dem all take dem nap.

An' folks in de swamp
say dat sometimes dey see
ol' Claude hangin' roun'
dat ol' stomp of a tree.

No Grand-Mère
No little girls
No cats !!!

DON' FEED
DIS →
GATOR!

No li.tHE
CAJUN girls
Allowed!

WERMS

PLEEZ Don'
Feed
AllyGATOR!

NO FEED
GATOR!

'Cause Claude, dat ol' gator,
he finally cool down.
But when he see people now,
he don' come roun'.

Ol' Claude reckon people
be too hot to eat.
He don' know dat de hot sauce
done made all de heat.

Ol' Claude, he been tricked,
so it all worked out good
fo' TeJean, Grand-mère,
an' Petite Rouge Riding Hood!